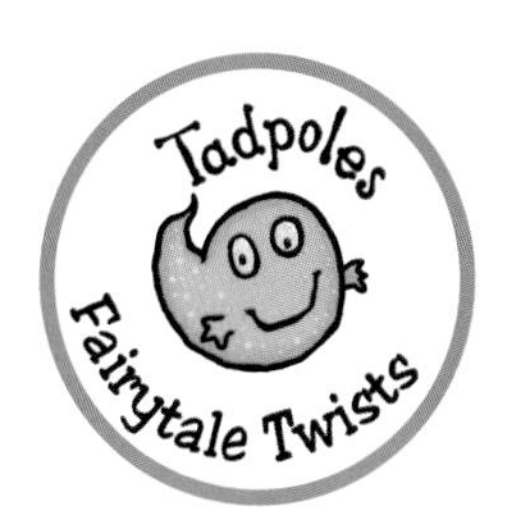

Hansel and Gretel and the Green Witch

Written by Laura North
Illustrated by Chris Jevons

Crabtree Publishing Company
www.crabtreebooks.com

Crabtree Publishing Company
www.crabtreebooks.com
1-800-387-7650

616 Welland Ave.
St. Catharines, ON
L2M 5V6

PMB 59051, 350 Fifth Ave.
59th Floor,
New York, NY 10118

Published by Crabtree Publishing in 2015

Series editor: Melanie Palmer
Editor: Kathy Middleton
Proofreader: Shannon Welbourn
Notes to adults: Reagan Miller
Series advisor: Catherine Glavina
Series designer: Peter Scoulding
Production coordinator and Prepress technician: Margaret Amy Salter
Print coordinator: Katherine Berti

First published in 2013 by Franklin Watts (A division of Hachette Children's Books)

Printed in Canada/022015/IH20141209

Library and Archives Canada Cataloguing in Publication

North, Laura, author
Hansel and Gretel and the green witch / written by Laura North ; illustrated by Chris Jevons.

(Tadpoles: fairytale twists)
Issued in print and electronic formats.
ISBN 978-0-7787-1928-1 (bound).--
ISBN 978-0-7787-1954-0 (pbk.).--
ISBN 978-1-4271-7692-9 (pdf).--
ISBN 978-1-4271-7684-4 (html)

I. Jevons, Chris, illustrator II. Title. III. Series: Tadpoles. Fairytale twists

PZ7.N815Ha 2015 j823'.9 C2014-907769-6
C2014-907770-X

Library of Congress Cataloging-in-Publication Data

CIP available at Library of Congress

This story is based on the traditional fairy tale, Hansel and Gretel, but with a new twist. Can you make up your own twist for the story?

Hansel and Gretel
liked to watch TV.

"What's on next, Hansel?" asked Gretel.

“I don’t know,” said Hansel.
“Pass the potato chips.”

Hansel and Gretel also liked to eat. They wolfed down cookies and gobbled cupcakes.

Their father, the woodcutter, was worried.

"My children will never move from that sofa."

One day, the woodcutter thought of a plan. “I will lay a trail of donuts to lead the children into the forest,” he said.

"They'll eat them all, and then they will have to get some exercise to make their way back home."

The donut trail lay gleaming in the sunlight, a cream-filled path with raspberry icing.

“Yum!” said Gretel. One by one, they ate the donuts leading them to the middle of the forest.

“It’s gotten dark,” said Hansel.

“I’m still hungry,” said Gretel, even though she had eaten 23 donuts.

Suddenly, they saw a house.
“I think it’s made of vegetables.
Yuk!” cried Gretel.

A witch suddenly appeared.
"Is that a donut?" she croaked.
"I like to eat children, but only active, healthy ones."

The children started to run, but the witch easily caught up with them.

First, she forced the children
to do an obstacle course.

"Please don't make us do any more exercise!" begged Hansel.

But the next day, she made them swim laps in the lake. "I can't swim another stroke," cried Gretel.

“Give me ten push-ups for complaining!” cried the witch.

On the third day, the witch made them jump over hurdles,

throw heavy iron balls,

...and run a half marathon.
“You’re starting to look
good enough to eat!”
she said, hungrily.

“I am so hungry I could eat a house!” said Gretel. She started tearing off part of the roof.

Hansel and Gretel ate the vegetable door, the vegetable chimney, and the vegetable table.

The children looked fit and healthy.

“Now you’re ready to be my dinner

said the witch.

But Hansel and Gretel were full of energy.

"You can't catch us!" they shouted, and they sped off quickly.

Hansel and Gretel ran all the way home. They told their father what had happened.

The woodcutter was glad to see them. “I’m sorry for sending you into the forest,” he said. “I just wanted you to get some exercise.”

That night, Hansel and Gretel turned the television off.

They cooked a big, healthy meal, made from bits of the witch's house they had taken with them.

Puzzle 1

Put these pictures in the correct order. Which event do you think is the most important? Now try writing the story in your own words

Puzzle 2

1. I am worried about my children.

2. I cook a lot of odd things!

3. We watch a lot of TV.

4. We hate doing any exercise.

5. I don't like to eat fat.

6. My job is to cut lots of wood.

Choose the correct speech bubbles for each character. Can you think of any others? Turn the page to find the answers for both pages.

Notes for adults

TADPOLES: Fairytale Twists are engaging, imaginative stories designed for early fluent readers. The books may also be used for read-alouds or shared reading with young children.

TADPOLES: Fairytale Twists are humorous stories with a unique twist on traditional fairy tales. Each story can be compared to the original fairy tale, or appreciated on its own. Fairy tales are a key type of literary text found in the Common Core State Standards.

THE FOLLOWING PROMPTS BEFORE, DURING, AND AFTER READING SUPPORT LITERACY SKILL DEVELOPMENT AND CAN ENRICH SHARED READING EXPERIENCES:

1. **Before Reading**: Do a picture walk through the book, previewing the illustrations. Ask the reader to predict what will happen in the story. For example, ask the reader what he or she thinks the twist in the story will be.
2. **During Reading**: Encourage the reader to use context clues and illustrations to determine the meaning of unknown words or phrases.
3. **During Reading**: Have the reader stop midway through the book to revisit his or her predictions. Does the reader wish to change his or her predictions based on what they have read so far?
4. **During and After Reading**: Encourage the reader to make different connections:
   Text-to-Text: How is this story similar to/different from other stories you have read?
   Text-to-World: How are events in this story similar to/different from things that happen in the real world?
   Text-to-Self: Does a character or event in this story remind you of anything in your own life?
5. **After Reading**: Encourage the child to reread the story and to retell it using his or her own words. Invite the child to use the illustrations as a guide.

HERE ARE OTHER TITLES FROM TADPOLES: FAIRYTALE TWISTS FOR YOU TO ENJOY:

Cinderella's Big Foot	978-0-7787-0440-9 RLB	978-0-7787-0448-5 PB
Jack and the Bean Pie	978-0-7787-0441-6 RLB	978-0-7787-0449-2 PB
Little Bad Riding Hood	978-0-7787-0442-3 RLB	978-0-7787-0450-8 PB
Princess Frog	978-0-7787-0443-0 RLB	978-0-7787-0452-2 PB
Rapunzel and the Prince of Pop	978-0-7787-1929-8 RLB	978-0-7787-1955-7 PB
Rumpled Stilton Skin	978-0-7787-1930-4 RLB	978-0-7787-1956-4 PB
Sleeping Beauty—100 Years Later	978-0-7787-0444-7 RLB	978-0-7787-0479-9 PB
Snow White Sees the Light	978-0-7787-1931-1 RLB	978-0-7787-1957-1 PB
The Elves and the Trendy Shoes	978-0-7787-1932-8 RLB	978-0-7787-1958-8 PB
The Emperor's New Uniform	978-0-7787-1933-5 RLB	978-0-7787-1959-5 PB
The Lovely Duckling	978-0-7787-0445-4 RLB	978-0-7787-0480-5 PB
The Pied Piper and the Wrong Song	978-0-7787-1934-2 RLB	978-0-7787-1960-1 PB
The Princess and the Frozen Peas	978-0-7787-0446-1 RLB	978-0-7787-0481-2 PB
The Three Frilly Goats Fluff	978-0-7787-1935-9 RLB	978-0-7787-1961-8 PB
The Three Little Pigs and the New Neighbor	978-0-7787-0447-8 RLB	978-0-7787-0482-9 PB

Answers

Puzzle 1

The correct order is: 1c, 2a, 3e, 4d, 5f, 6b

Puzzle 2

Hansel and Gretel: 3, 4;
The woodcutter: 1, 6; The witch: 2, 5